TelTel Series

The Prayerful Woman

Book Two

TelTel Series

The Prayerful Woman

Book Two

K.B. Onyango

Published by Sahel Publishing Association,
a subsidiary of Sahel Books Inc.
P.O. Box 18007—00100
Nairobi, Kenya
Tel: +011-254-715-596-106
For questions and orders log on to:
www.sahelpublishing.net

A Sahel Book
Nairobi. New Delhi. London. Nashville.
Editor: Sam Okello
Interior design and cover by Hellen Wahonya Okello
Images: Courtesy google.com
Printed in India

This book is dedicated to my children Junior, Michelle and Hadassah

Acknowledgement

Writing a short story collection so soon after another is as taxing an experience as it is deeply rewarding. I had to do it this way to answer the many questions my colleagues and friends were asking. The main question was: *We have little ones and teenagers in our homes. You wrote a good book for the little ones, what about the teenagers?*

The Prayerful Woman is the answer I have for that question.

May I acknowledge the following people for their assistance in completing this book in a very short time:

- My family members, who kept checking on me as I burnt my midnight oil.
- My colleagues and friends, who asked for a teenage book.
- My publisher, who stopped everything else in order to beat their earlier record in publishing *The Dance Party*.

May the lessons in these stories be a blessing to the reader!

Table of Contents

One

THE PRAYERFUL WOMAN

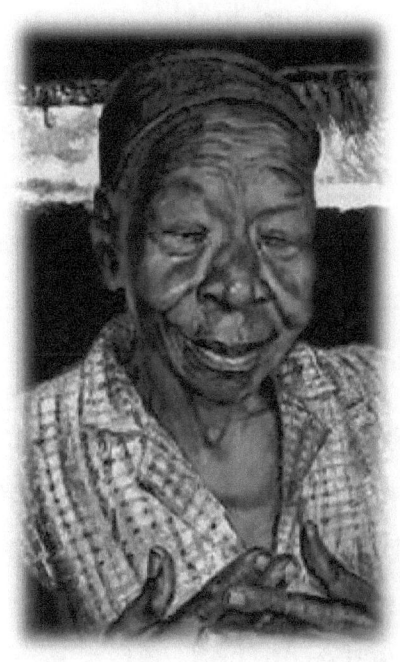

Many years ago, in the village of Kilong', there was a widow called Damar. Her husband died at a young age, leaving her with the difficult task of bringing up their three children—a boy and two girls. The children were named after the months they were born. The first was named Aprilla, followed by June and lastly Augustine, the boy. At the time her husband died, Augustine was only three months old. The girls were aged four and two respectively. Like every woman in the village, she went about her businesses, including working in the gardens, drawing water, fetching firewood and preparing meals for her children.

With little support from her extended family, the children were able to go to the local primary school like other children of their age. Without good school uniforms, school levies and required books, they were on and off school, but they progressed anyway.

Back at home, life was equally difficult. Their mother could hardly provide enough. On several nights they went to bed on empty stomachs. And since there was nothing to eat before bed, there would be nothing for breakfast as well, the following morning. Even if there was, there would be no time to prepare and to take it.

School days were particularly difficult. Their school was very far. This meant waking up very early and running all the way to school so as to reach on time. In those days, school children would be instructed to bring firewood for the teachers, and after games they would fetch water for the teachers, among other chores, before the day ended.

Then there was manual work in the morning. On arrival, there was general cleaning of the school compound before going to class. In class, teachers had no way of knowing their pupils' problems. All they did was to teach and call it a day.

There was this Mathematics teacher who did not let those who could not solve his sums go for lunch. He always asked a few mental sums to warm up his students before embarking on the day's work. He was popular and unpopular at the same time, because of his habit of shouting the day's warm up questions before reaching the class. It went something like this:

> I'm thinking of a number, multiply it by five, subtract three and the answer is twenty seven.

He said these words before reaching the classroom door. Only "what is the number?" was asked at the doorway.

Then there was this History teacher who was really funny. There was this time he taught about the Great Trek. Lost in the glory of the subject at hand, he chose to demonstrate how the traders walked. He said, "Those traders walked and walked and walked...." As he said the word walked and walked, he literally went around the classroom, demonstrating how the traders walked. It was so much drama!

When the bell rang to end the lesson, he wobbled to the front of the class and said, "Oh! I have really taught today!"

With time, these children got used to eating one meal a day and that was supper. Weekends were a welcome break because there was a day to catch a break from the tight weekday routine. But it also meant helping their mother with gardening and other domestic chores.

With all these difficulties, God was kind to this family health-wise and they never fell sick. Not even the common cold seemed to know this family existed. These were the days public health matters were not known. Of course there were health centers in every location, but those locations were the size of today's divisions or sub counties. This meant that most people lived far from health facilities.

This brought about a unique problem—the quack health technician, popularly called "Doctor." It was common to find a class four dropout moving from home to home treating the sick. The quack would carry a bag with all sorts of instruments and one syringe and needle.

When he arrived to treat a sick person, the first thing he asked for was hot water for cleaning the needle and syringe. As he cleaned, the "Doctor" would jet the hot water from the syringe, drawing several *eights* on the mud walls as if to say "it is eight times clean!"

If one child was sick, all the other children in the family would also be injected to prevent the disease from spreading to them. And since he had only one syringe and one needle, after every injection he cleaned the tools in the same way in readiness to inject another patient.

In those days everybody seemed to believe that if one was not given an injection he or she was only half treated. Through some miracle, these patients became well soon after treatment.

———

These children grew up knowing that life was a struggle. The first time the eldest of the two girls, Aprilla, ever had something under her feet was when her aunt asked her to help with the luggage to catch a bus. Aprilla helped the aunt carry the bag, prompting the aunt to reward her with a pair of bathroom slippers.

Aprilla girl was too happy to put on the slippers. She had to carry the pair in her hand as packed and ran all the way home. The slippers were carefully kept and were worn only when there was an occasion that necessitated such dressing.

Since one of their aunts had given Aprilla slippers, June, her sister, now believed that only aunts gave slippers. So one day she hatched a trick to get her own pair.

They had another aunt, Lilian, who lived in the direction where the sun set. Each time this aunt visited, she was warm, kind, nice and made Damar's family very happy. *The best thing to do is to run to Aunty Lilian's home one day and come back with my own pair of slippers*, June thought.

Because Lilian usually set off in the afternoon for her journey back home, June thought her home must not be too far away. So this afternoon, June ran away with the hope of visiting Lilian and eventually getting her own pair of slippers.

Back at home, Aprilla and Augustine looked for June for hours but couldn't find her. They looked at the homes of neighbours, uncles, grandparents and school mates, but she was nowhere to be found.

All this time their mother had gone to the market to do shopping for Easter celebrations. On her arrival from the market, she met the visibly disturbed and gloomy children. On learning that June had disappeared and the efforts her children had made to trace her had so far been unsuccessful, she was lost for words. Her reaction was a shocker to her two girls. She called them inside the house, closed the door and told each of them to pray to God. She trusted God to take care of her missing daughter.

In the meantime June walked and walked and walked. She got very tired and it was approaching sunset. She was lost and everybody who met her was asking her one question: Young girl, where are you going?

With no proper answer, a follow up question was: Where have you come from?

All June did was cry instead of providing an answer to the questions. She was lost and everyone around was a stranger. And to make matters worse, she could not trace her way back home.

She was lonely because that was the first time an evening found her away from her mother and siblings. It was bad and really scary!

An elderly lady offered to accommodate her for the night. It was fast getting dark and the way she was crying, she needed a lot of understanding.

The lady said, "Come on, young girl, follow me to my house. Let us go so you can rest till tomorrow, then I can help you find your way back to your home."

June hesitated at first.

The lady said, "Let us go now because my granddaughter at home may be worried just like you are."

The people at the scene promised to come to the lady's home and assist June get back home the following morning. June obliged and followed the old lady to her house.

Back at home, June's siblings could not eat their supper. It was the first time June was away at night and they did not know where she was. It was Good Friday but the evening was not that good for them without June.

Mama and her two sad girls started to worry because June had not been seen in the neighbourhood. Did someone steal her? Did she die? What had happened to June?

At about a half past seven, that evening, Mother again called her children and told them to pray before darkness set in so that God could take care of them and June, wherever she was. She assured them that with God their sister was safe and would come back before the next school day. They prayed together, struggled to eat, then had a sleepless night.

Where June was accommodated, word went round that grandmother had come home with a visitor. Some of her grandchildren came to greet the visitor. The children were happy it was Easter and they had a visitor.

It was a particularly joyous moment because she was young, so they would play together. Unfortunately, the visitor was unhappy. She looked very sad despite the spirited efforts of her hosts to comfort her.

One of the children ran back to her house and told her mother about the visitor and how gloomy she was.

Moments later, someone knocked on the door. It was about a half past eight in the evening. "Who is it?" asked Grandmother.

"Mother, it's me, Lilian," came the answer.

Grandmother knew the voice well. It was her daughter-in-law and the mother of her favourite granddaughter, who had been in her house a while ago.

She rushed to open the door.

When the door swung open, Lilian noticed someone sitting in the house, so she asked who the visitor was.

Grandmother said, "I don't know her yet. She's been crying all evening even after I assured her I'll help her find her way back home tomorrow."

Lilian felt it was smart to greet the visitor; maybe that would provide a little comfort. She greeted the girl from the doorway.

She said, "Good evening my daughter......"

The visitor ran to the door without an answer. And within seconds, there was confusion in the house as she jumped and held onto Lilian's arm saying, "Aunty, Aunty, I found you...!"

With those words, everybody felt relieved and Lilian was happy to see her niece.

All Grandmother could say was, "Are you staying here or going with Aunty?"

June went with her aunt and spent the night in her house!

———

Many years later, after Damar's children were through with school and were taking care of their own families, she was cooking in her kitchen.

It was in the evening and as usual in this part of the world, doors were left ajar or shut, not bolted, for the evening. This was to allow the chicken to come to roost. There was not a single security threat and nobody could remember when anything had ever been stolen to warrant locking the doors. Furthermore, why would a village widow worry about anything?

In the village, Damar was considered lucky and blessed. Her daughters were married to families of class and her only son had a good job in the city. The three children had combined their savings and helped put up a decent house for their mother, complete with a water tank and a solar system to light the home. Everybody in the village agreed that since she was a Christian of good standing, God had answered her prayers and was using her to send a message to the village. Her blessings were the talk of the village!

This evening, just like all others, looked normal. Damar prepared her meal and ate it in the kitchen. She sang praise songs and thanked God for being kind to her. She thanked the Lord for being her shepherd and a good provider for her needs. She kept referring to how God had helped the Israelites out of Egypt all the way to Canaan, and how the Lord would help His people to the Promised Land. Unknown to her, a thug had sneaked into her house armed with a sharp machete. The thug had been hired by a neighbor to kill her that night. This neighbor was just envious; he had nothing against this poor widow.

Damar shut her door at eight o'clock and knelt to pray. She sang a praise song, then started to pray. It was a Friday evening and this was how she prayed.

> Oh God, Lord of Hosts. Here I kneel before thee to express my gratitude for the week you gave me. You allowed me to do my work and guided my feet not to tumble at all. Thank you for guiding my mouth and preventing me from quarrelling with anybody. If I wronged someone,

forgive me and teach me how to forgive those who wronged me. I do not want to carry any grudge into the Holy Sabbath. I am only a woman far from being perfect and only you, Father, may cleanse me.

I want to pray for my children wherever they are, Lord. Thank you for Aprilla and her family. May your light shine through her and guide her ways. Let her trust you in everything she does.

Remember June as well, Lord. You know her needs. As she goes about her business, be with her in all that she does. I pray for her journeys, her happy and sad moments; be her refuge and shield.

I pray for my only son, Augustine, Father. Show him your kindness and unending love. In his duties, be his Alpha and Omega. Let him put you first and last and trust only your wisdom. Remember his young family and show all my children your ways every day, dear Lord.

For those who did not get something to eat today, Father, be with them. For the sick, kindly heal them. For the bereaved, kindly console them in your special way, Father. Those who are travelling, to them grant journey mercies.

For my neigbours and the entire village, grant us brotherly love and peace. May we live as one family in Christ. Let us be our brothers' keepers always.

For those possessed by the power of darkness, deliver them, dear Lord. Those who steal, Father, help them find other means of living.

Those who kill by the gun or sword, Father, soften their hearts so they may know that the people they kill are your children. And those who hire others to kill, teach them your ways, Lord.

This night, dear Lord, I trust you will touch someone's heart and he will leave his bad ways and start praising you. I ask you, dear Lord, for a safe night as we celebrate this Sabbath. Send your angels to protect us this night so we may wake up to praise you tomorrow.

She said amen!

The thug came out of his hiding and ordered Damar to sit. She sat and the thug told her not to worry. "I was hired by your neighbour to kill you but your prayer touched me. Here is the machete I would have used to cut your head and here is part of the money I was given. It was Baba Mkwenge who sent me, but leave him to God. May that Lord you serve take care of you."

Damar whispered, *Thank you, Lord!*

The thug said, "Open the door so I can leave".

She opened the door and the thug melted away in the darkness outside. She shut her door again, said a silent prayer and went to bed.

Two

THE DARING MADMAN

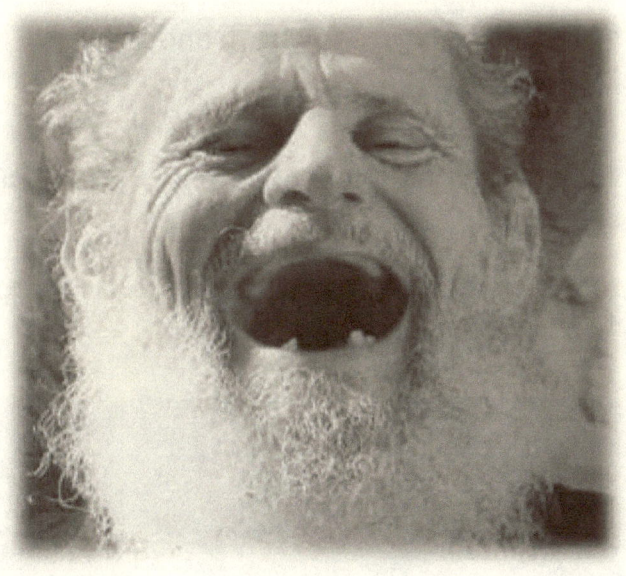

In a remote part of a country called Tima, there was a village known as Moko. People from Moko were peace-loving and lived like one big family. It was a village with a unique family structure, where everyone was related to everyone as grandparent, parent, brother or sister, uncle or aunt, son or daughter, grandchild, brother-in-law or sister-in-law. It was wonderful to hear stories about the village.

But every river has its snakes and every market has its madman. Moko had its madman too. The man was a weakling, who thought playing tough would make people fear him.

The villagers, though, ignored him and asked him to join soldiers in the World War if he thought he was tougher than other men in the village. To many, he was just a madman.

Parties were the order of the day in the village. A villager slaughtering a bull for the village to party was not a surprise. And in turns they did it, from time to time. Each time there was a party this madman came and insisted he be given a piece of meat to roast. For the sake of peace, he would be given and the merrymaking would not be interrupted.

He got used to doing that and at times he would demand a bigger piece or he would drive cooks out of the kitchen to roast his piece first. This did not auger well with the young men in the village. The young men thought he needed a life lesson, but the right opportunity had not presented itself for this lesson, so the madman went on disrupting peace from time to time.

The Swahili saying that *Races on the floor end at the wall* must have had a deeper meaning for the madman. In one such party, he asked for meat and the young men told him off. He was told to slaughter his own bull and share the meat; after all he had been given a lot of unnecessary attention in the past. A standoff followed that nearly ended the party.

On seeing how serious the young men were, the madman decided his ego had been badly bruised. He declared war on the entire village, especially on the young men. Since he had no weapon ready, he made a simple statement.

He said, "I'll be back," and off he went.

To his threat, one of the young men responded, "You better go for good."

As he left for his home, which was barely a kilometer away, he was disturbed. Deep in his heart was a wound. *How can these fools tell me to go for good from the family party? Am I not one of them? I must do something!* He went to his house and got his arsenal. He came out with a spear, two clubs and a machete.

Back at the party, the young men were also disturbed. One of them called a small meeting and the young men decided to teach the madman a lesson should he return. They knew that together they were much stronger than him.

They were back doing their routine chores for the party as they pondered what to do with this man—to end his errant behaviour.

"Tie him to that tree over there," said one.

"No, several strokes of the cane will drive the madness off his head," said another.

Before the third one gave his opinion, a woman shouted, "Run for your lives, he is coming with a..." and took off before completing what she was about to say. The madman went after her in hot pursuit.

The rest of the merrymakers thought it was a joke. The woman was heard pleading for her life when the madman suddenly seemed to remember he'd had an issue with the young men, not the woman. He left the woman alone and ran towards one of the houses in the homestead. He dared any of them to come out and fight him. Since he was armed, no one came out.

He decided to go for those in the house. Everybody scampered for safety in a corner, crying at the top of their voices. Meanwhile, from another house, someone ran out and the madman followed him briefly.

Seconds later, the madman turned and headed for the house, where more male voices were. He kicked the door open and the cry was even louder. People covered themselves with a mat so they would not see the madman spear them.

In the meantime, more people escaped from the other houses, including the young men who had told him off. He spotted them just in time and started to go after one of the young men.

The commotion was heard in surrounding villages, prompting young men to come—to find out why the madman was chasing people.

On seeing a large crowd gathering, the mad man slipped into a bush and disappeared. By this time he had spent much time chasing and scaring people, but no one was hurt.

People were furious upon learning the reason this fellow was causing mayhem in the village. In the meantime the meat, which was cooking, got burnt. Remaining portions of the meat turned into a party for dogs. The young men, who had wanted to teach the man a lesson, ended up being taught a lesson themselves.

Later, an old man from the neighbouring village called a small gathering to order. He declared the village to be inhabited by women. "No one should claim to be a man here. You are all women," he said. "How can one man cause life to stall in this village? Where is that madman right now?" he demanded.

On being told where the madman was last seen, he took charge. "Take no weapons and follow me. Be vigilant and check any signs. Alert me if you see him."

A short while later, he asked everybody in his group to pick small stones. "Pick not less than four and let us go."

They all did.

"We will all throw these stones in one go when I command, then let us see what follows. Ensure you remain with at least a stone, should none hit the man. His arsenal will be nothing compared to ours," the old man said.

When the madman saw this small group coming, he roared out of the bush and charged at them. He noted that these people were not armed. He thought they would be scared, but no one seemed shaken, which troubled him.

He charged on, but on reaching thirty meters from the group, the old man ordered, "Hit him!"

Stones rained on the madman, causing him to fall to the ground face down.

"He is dead!" shouted one of the stone throwers.

He lay still, with his arsenal scattered all over the place. For five straight minutes everything was quiet. Everybody waited anxiously to throw another stone should he move, but the old man told them to wait as he checked the condition of the madman.

As the old man approached the madman, the madman rose to his feet, ran and fell on the old man, pleading for his life. He must have been waiting for this moment. He had judged, while on the ground, that showing any sign of life would have proved fatal. But even as he held on to the old man, he bled on.

The old man had to do something. Only he stood between the madman and death. As fate had it, respect for the old man made nobody throw another stone. Like an earring to the ear, the madman didn't let go of him. From that day on, the madman changed his ways and taught the young never to play tough.

Three

THE ROUGH PREFECT

In a remote part of Bigiri, there lived a peasant farmer, with his family. This family had seven children—six daughters and one son. The son was born after three girls, so he had three more sisters after him. His name was Charles and everybody fondly called him Charlie. The girls loved their only brother so dearly because he was bright in school. Charlie was shy and did not talk much. He was small in body, but his heart was giant. When offended, he would dare anybody to a fight. As things turned out, nobody wanted to fight him, so most of the time he had his way.

By the time Charlie finished primary school he had grown horns. He was on top of the world, and given that he was good in class made things even better for him.

He did well and was happy to have completed primary education at a young age. And luck was on his side because when primary school results were announced later in the year, he was among the best performing candidates in his Division.

Charlie was called to a national school, but his parents could not afford to pay the school fees. He was sent to form one in a local day school. In the end of term examinations, he did so well and instantly became every teacher's darling. He was soon made the class prefect.

When Charlie's distant uncle heard of his good work in school, the uncle offered to pay his school fees. Charlie requested for change of schools and promised to get straight As in all subjects if he could join a provincial school.

The uncle obliged and joined the search for a school where Charlie could join form two the following year. It was not easy, but luck was on his side. One headmaster gave Charlie a chance. This headmaster looked at the primary exam marks, the fact that Charlie had been called to a national school, and that he had consistently scored high marks in form one. These were enough reasons to admit the boy to form two straight away.

Those were the days when bullying in schools was almost official. Form ones, popularly known as *monos*, were inducted into schools through various forms of bullying. In some cases, they swept and cleaned all loos, dormitories and did all the menial work. Use of foul language on them, by other students, was the order of the day.

Indeed, in some schools, teachers encouraged bullying. There was a case of a headmaster who would keep warning form ones in his school that one day he would let the form twos "dehorn them." The message was clear!

In Charlie's previous school, this was not the case because each student came from around the school, and thus all the students had known one another before coming to the school.

As was his desire, Charlie reported to form two in a new school. Teachers in his former school were happy that in a provincial school he would meet bright boys like him and that would help improve his grades. One thing awaited him, though—induction to the new school, known as bullying.

There were a few other boys who joined Charlie's new school that same year, but unlike

Charlie, most of them came from boarding schools, where they had been bullied already. They knew how to find their way around the bullying circles, so they coped quite well. Charlie could not understand why anybody would call him a "mono" when he was in form two.

He got angry, but being new he could do nothing about it. He burnt with anger day after day. When examinations were done, he was among the top in his class. This impressed his new teachers and caught the attention of all the boys in the school. He thus acquired a new name: The Sharp Newcomer.

After a while, Charlie was made a prefect. His class became the quietest and most orderly because whenever he forwarded the names of noisemakers, he made sure they were punished. His classmates kept quiet and got to class on time to avoid problems with Charlie.

Because of the discipline in his class, teachers thought Charlie was such a good prefect. By the end of form three, he was made the school head boy. His classmates were not amused because they knew a number of boys would be sent home.

Probably recalling how he had been bullied when he joined the school, Charlie went on a revenge mission. He became unreasonable and would not understand anything anyone told him. His behavior bordered on haughtiness.

There was this case where the teacher on duty sent a boy to call the head cook, but upon meeting the boy, Charlie ordered him back to class. This boy followed the teacher's instructions, went ahead and called the head cook and by the time he ran to class, the headmaster had sent the school secretary to call him, ready with a suspension letter.

It took the teacher on duty's intervention to save this boy from suspension.

Charlie took his duties so seriously that his performance in class started going down. Things went from bad to worse. By mid form four, he was in the bottom quarter of the class.

One day there was this boy who Charlie caught talking in mother tongue. When Charlie asked why, the boy said, "Charlie, what's the big deal, even you can't match me in English." And he said it in mother tongue!

This earned the boy suspension from school.

By the time the final examinations were done, Charlie had made enough enemies and could not even sleep in the dormitory. He spent the night in the headmaster's house, fearing he could be attacked at night.

But spending nights in headmaster's house only postponed the problem because the boys plotted how to get him out of school. Add this to the fact that he was not doing well in class,

Charlie did not perform well in end of secondary school examinations.

Back at home, everyone was expecting straight As in all subjects from their bright and only boy. But when Charlie came home after the exams he looked worried. After pleas from his mother, he said he did not do the exams well so he feared he would not perform well. They prayed together and left matters in the hands of the Lord.

But for Charlie, the damage was done. A school is a place where people from everywhere meet so if one makes enemies there he becomes a public enemy and that is exactly what happened. Charlie could not visit his relatives because he feared running into an enemy from school. Public gatherings became a no go zone!

When results were later announced, Charlie could not even go to pick his. His father went to pick results on his behalf.

After many years at home, luck finally smiled and Charlie secured a job as a security guard. He was posted to guard the senior quarters of a big factory in the city. All senior staffers here were allocated a home, complete with a gate. Charlie was assigned gate number seven.

The guards who had been previously assigned to this Manager praised him for his kind gestures to them. He provided a thermos full of tea to the guard on duty every evening. Even drivers praised this Manager. No one complained about him. Charlie, aware of the man's kindness, counted himself lucky to be assigned to his gate.

Charlie reported to work one evening and soon the Manager was dropped off in his official car. The Manager greeted him, "Good evening, Askari—Guard?"

Charlie said, "Good evening, Sir".

That evening, like all the others, tea was brought. In the house the Manager was told their usual guard was transferred and a new one had taken charge. This Manager had no problem with that because transfers, he knew, were a normal occurrence in dynamic organizations.

In this company, the names of Managers were written on the gate. In the morning, Charlie was replaced by the day guard, but he had noted the name. And though He left before the Manager was out of the house, one thing was sure—it could not have been a coincidence. The name sounded familiar.

On the second day the Manager came earlier from work and was stunned to see his old school head boy, who had punished him daily back in school. *But how could it be?* he wondered.

As he entered the gate, Charlie greeted the Manager, but the man did not answer. One look at Charlie and he disappeared into the house.

The Manager called his family together and asked details of the new night guard. Every detail fitted his former head boy.

He said, "Look, together with his tea, give him supper as well." After saying that, he went to bed, never eating anything.

The following morning this troubled Manager went to the Security Manager's office and sought replacement of his night guard. The Security Manager wondered what the poor guard had done in just two days. Right then, his phone rang. It was a call from the security firm's Operations Manager. He wanted to know what had happened that had caused the guard to ask for transfer in just two days, yet everybody was sad when they were transferred from this Manager's residence.

It later emerged that while both had no problems with each other right now, past events, those from high school, could not allow Charlie to guard this Manager.

Four

THE SCHOOL GHOST

There are schools all over the place with funny stories. These stories range from how the land on which the school stands was acquired to a unique event that took place in the school. The older and bigger a school, the more the number and the funnier those stories are.

In the days of those old schools, every student in a secondary school was a celebrity in his village. Boys in class four were old enough to shave and reaching class five was no mean feat for a girl. Many girls got married upon finishing lower primary. In class three, a girl had had enough education to take care of a family. Those are the days a teacher was considered a senior government officer.

Those days, a cheque was so rare to come by that every student paid fees in cash. It was common to carry fees stashed in the socks. There were no one thousand shilling notes and the highest denomination available was the one hundred shilling note.

There was only one bus that plied the route of this school and if one missed it, there was no option but to postpone a trip to the following day. Tarmac roads were few and electricity was only available in big towns. The buses looked like a loaf of bread.

Those days, schools with telephone lines were few and even if a school had one, most of the time the line was dead—and when it was alive, making a call was a problem because the lines were not clear. The caller had to shout at the top of his or her voice to be heard by the other person on line.

Those days, the education system distinguished secondary schools from high schools because the later had forms five and six while the former had up to form four only. Those in form five and six wore long trousers and a blazer while those in lower forms wore short trousers and a pullover.

Those days, secondary school education meant a bright future even when one reached form two and sat junior secondary school examinations only.

There is this story of an imaginary school ghost that haunted boys in a leading school in the Mboika area. Rumour had it that the ghost started haunting this famous school in the early part of the 1970s.

When the school opened for term two and the boys reported with their fees, the headmaster personally collected the money. He did that daily for the first week of the term and going by the number of students, he must have collected a good sum of money.

In most cases he took the week's collection to the bank, which was tens of kilometers away. Since the largest denomination was one hundred shilling note and the collection was done for a whole week, it took a long time to serve one customer at the bank, especially a headmaster coming with two or three bags of money.

Smart thieves must have known that schools had money in the first two weeks of opening. One time, on the third night of the opening week, thieves came to steal from this school. They cut open the fence from a dark corner and came to the gate, where they held the watchmen on duty and tied their hands, legs and mouths. They broke the headmaster's door and entered.

While this was going on, a couple of students had woken up to do private study using their lanterns. They came quietly and entered the classroom next to the headmaster's office. Before long, they heard the sound of things falling. Then they heard the sound of something like a metal box being opened. One of the boys ran back to the dormitory to call others.

The boys came with all kinds of weapons: slashers, hoes, blunt wood, hockey sticks....

As they ran towards the administration block, the thieves sensed danger and ran away, but one of the thieves hid himself among the empty cartons in the headmaster's office. The boys gave a good chase, but the thieves disappeared into the bushy maize fields. It became impossible to catch them after they ran out of the school compound.

As those who gave chase came back, they found the watchmen tied behind the generator room. The headmaster was called from his house to see for himself.

When the generator was started and the office checked, the outer door was broken, right to his desk. And while they were still assessing the loss, something moved and the cowards took off.

But one boy shouted, "Somebody is here!"

They moved the cartons and the thief started pleading for mercy. And that was when the boys went mad. He was pulled out of hiding and beaten mercilessly outside the office. Pleas from the headmaster only managed to calm the noise, but not the beating. After an hour or so, the thief was declared dead under a heap of stones. Police were called the following morning and they took the body away.

A week later, a joke started doing rounds in the school. The boys nicknamed the dead thief Okok. Whenever a boy fell sick, it was the ghost of Okok haunting him. If someone did poorly in exams, it was Okok. Okok became the cause of all problems in the school.

When new boys joined the school, Okok's story was told to them. They were told that Okok was only seen at midnight and not at other times. His body was not seen, but his white gum boots were—as he walked around the compound. It was dangerous to be outside the dormitory during those hours because Okok would avenge his death, they were told. The boys became fearful and no one wanted to be out of the dormitory during those hours.

On a chilly night, many years later, one of the boys was pressed during the night so he said to himself, "Let me go for a short call, Okok is not waiting for me out there!"

When he opened the door, he discovered that there were others also suffering in silence. One of them joined the first boy and go out. The second boy found military boots belonging to his friend and put them on. As he rushed towards the door, the first boy, who was already outside the dormitory, heard the footsteps and thought Okok was coming for him!

He dashed back to the dormitory only to collide head-on with the second boy. The first boy let out a loud cry, "Okok is taking my life!"

In the mix up, the second boy got up and ran back towards his bed.

The sound of his boots in the corridor, coupled with the first boy's scream, sent panic through the entire dormitory.

The second boy run to his bed but missed it. He jumped on another boy, who yelled hysterically while moving out of his bed.

In the next few minutes, it became the terrible noise of "Okok is killing us" from the dormitory. One watchman ran and started the generator. As lights came on, most of the boys were seen hiding under their beds. The lights remained on till morning.

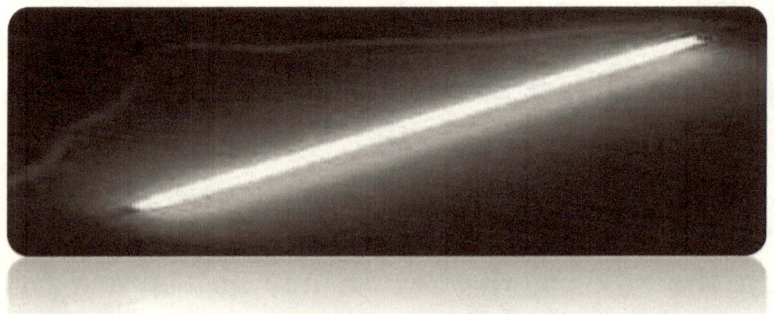

Everybody in the school got scared and teachers were called to a crisis meeting in the morning. Nobody wanted lights off ever again for fear of the return of Okok; and most boys requested to be transferred to other schools. By ten o'clock, nobody talked about any other matters.

It was Okok!

In the afternoon the dormitory master called a meeting of his boys. He said he wanted to arrest Okok in broad daylight so he could leave the boys in peace.

He brought a chair, sat in the middle of the dormitory and asked everybody to sit on his bed. He assured the boys that no one would be sent home even if they were wrong, but Okok had to be sent away for good!

He asked the boys if they knew the person who was attacked by Okok.

Everybody remained silent, but on assurance that no records would be taken, one boy raised his hand. He narrated how he had gone for a short call and heard footsteps. He ran back and collided with someone in the corridor. He screamed, got up and ran, but missed his bed and jumped on another boy, who also yelled...

At that point, the teacher saw another hand raised and interrupted the new boy.

The second boy started giving his side of the story. He said he was also pressed and when he heard someone head towards the door, he looked for his slippers, but got the military boots, which he put on and walked towards the door. As he walked, something hit him hard and he ran back to his bed, but found someone on it... at this stage everybody was laughing so loudly and uncontrollably.

After ten minutes of hysterical laughter, they all agreed they had found Okok and that there was no reason to change dormitories or school. They agreed to protect the identity of those affected and soon it was smiles in the dormitory and the school. Today the story lives on, but the fear of Okok is no more.

Five

ANSWERED PRAYERS

In a village called Kilomele, in a country called Kamoro, lived a Preacher. Some people called him God's Messenger; others called him Pastor, Preacher, Evangelist, Priest, Prophet and many other titles. But those titles aside, he was a man of God. So powerful were his messages that everywhere he went, he earned great following and many people turned to God.

He travelled far and wide preaching the gospel and left a mark. He could pass for the legendary missionary who came to a village and found no Christian and when he left there was no pagan.

One time he visited the Western part of the country. It seemed God's Word was needed in this area more than the towns and cities, where crusaders and street preachers had pitched camp and claimed territories.

In the village, people believed in witchcraft. One could not set off on a journey without consulting the 'wise', as they were popularly known. Before this preacher came to the village, his coming was made known and was assessed as safe by the wise men and women of the village.

Two weeks before the great preacher's arrival, something strange happened in the village. Given proximity of the village to a world-known game park, a lone elephant strayed into the village. The elephant attacked residents and domestic animals, necessitating game rangers to shoot it. The village greeted news of the shooting with unparalleled jubilation. The fact that the body of a huge bull elephant laid still in the village made people receive calls from far and wide.

The villagers here were a superstitious lot. They believed in mystical powers "vested" in elephant parts. Phones rang all day and it was just a matter of time before it was all systems go. Relatives from far, and even abroad, called to ask for specific parts of the animal.

Stronger members of the village were paid to secure at least a piece for those who couldn't secure a piece on their own.

When night fell, people got ready with their tools and crude weapons—to secure a piece of this mystical animal. Within two hours, only the skull and large bones remained.

Later, the preacher arrived. Many people came to welcome him. He was received with great joy. And since posters had been placed everywhere and everybody was looking forward to seeing this man of God, the village was not going to be same again. That was the feeling.

Only a few days earlier, the carcass of a large elephant had caused villagers to act in an ungodly manner. Perhaps God had tried the villagers by letting their sinful and wicked minds to be exposed by the death of the elephant. To many staunch Christians, God wanted the village to come back to Him!

That week, a number of powerful sermons and songs were experienced. Even those who had never set foot in the nearby churches attended. Many seriously considered converting from their faiths to this new faith. Indeed, some must have made up their minds, but had not gone public about joining the new faith.

The climax of the revival week was to be on the last Sunday. There would be a great service in which all manner of problems were going to be solved. The sick would be healed, the mute would talk for the first time and the crippled would walk. After all Jesus said, "Come oh ye that are heavy laden and I will give you rest." The village was really ready for this great

Sunday and people were ready with their many problems. Salvation had come!

On Sunday, the sick formed the largest group of those in attendance. Their hope was to get well after the intercessory prayers.

Alongside those who came on their own were those who were brought by their relatives. There were as many problems as those in attendance. The poor came with the hope that they would be rich. Then there were those who came only to see what would happen at the service. Those who did not attend this prayer meeting must have been a handful.

The man of God was ready and the service started. The message touched many hearts and it appeared like the Lord wanted many in the village to change their ways. Many remembered how, only few days earlier, they had fought for and kept vital elephant organs in their houses. Now this man of God was saying that pieces of that giant elephant were of no use against witchdoctors; that only Jesus was!

When he uttered the words, "Come ye who are heavy laden," many were touched. He called the sick and said, "Even the crippled can receive legs and walk here and now. Whatever the problem come and the Lord will give you rest!"

Soon a man on a wheelchair was wheeled to the front.

People became curious about him.

In this village there had never been anybody on a wheelchair. But since it was a spiritual day and the coming of the man of God had spread to surrounding villages, somebody must have brought a physically challenged relative here to be healed.

In the crowd there was also an elderly woman. Moved by the man on the wheelchair, she thought to herself, "I will carry my load and give it to Jesus."

She carried her sack and made it to the front. She was in tears as she spoke through an interpreter to the man of God. And there were seven people in front by the time she came forward.

She said, "Let Jesus save me. I have had this for forty years and am tired. Pray for me so that I can be free!"

As she talked, a giant snake slithered from the sack and the man of God was the first to take off, followed by the "crippled man" on the wheelchair. The interpreter followed suit and within a second, the poor lady remained alone in front. Most of the people sitting in front also ran in different directions and the snake was gone never to be seen again.

That marked the sad end of a successful crusade by the "Man of God."